BASHO
and the
FOX

by Tim Myers • illustrated by Oki S. Han

Marshall Cavendish
New York • London • Singapore

To Cilla and Cassie, Seth and Nick—sweeter
than late-summer cherries.

—T. M.

For J. C., my son Joseph and Mom in Heaven

—O. S. H.

Text copyright © 2000 by Tim Myers
Illustrations copyright © 2000 by Oki S. Han
All rights reserved
Marshall Cavendish, 99 White Plains Road, Tarrytown, NY 10591
www.marshallcavendish.com

Library of Congress Cataloging-in-Publication Data
Myers, Tim.
Basho and the fox / by Tim Myers ; illustrated by Oki S. Han.
   p.   cm.
Summary: A famous Japanese poet is challenged by a fox to create his best haiku. ISBN: 0-7614-5190-0
1. Matsuo, Basho, 1644-1694—Juvenile fiction. [1. Matsuo, Basho, 1644-1694—Fiction.
2. Foxes—Fiction. 3. Poetry—Fiction.] I. Han, Oki, S., ill. II. Title.
PZ7.M9919   Bas   2000   [E]—dc21   99-054755

The text of this book is set in 14 point Meridien.
The illustrations are rendered in watercolor.
Printed in China
First Marshall Cavendish paperback edition
6   5   4   3   2   1

PREFACE

Basho is one of Japan's greatest poets. He lived in the 1600s and wrote many beautiful haiku and other works.

A haiku is a short poem that usually has only seventeen syllables. But in those few syllables you can sometimes see and feel what the poet saw and felt, as if you'd been there at that very moment. Basho's second poem in this story—about a frog jumping into a pond—is simple. But it sets a very powerful mood—and it's probably the most famous haiku ever written.

This is my own story about Basho, who, according to what we know, was not only a great poet, but also a very open-hearted man.

Long ago in Japan, the great poet Basho lived for a time like a hermit in Fukagawa. There he ate his food, slept his sleep, lived his life, and wrote his poems.

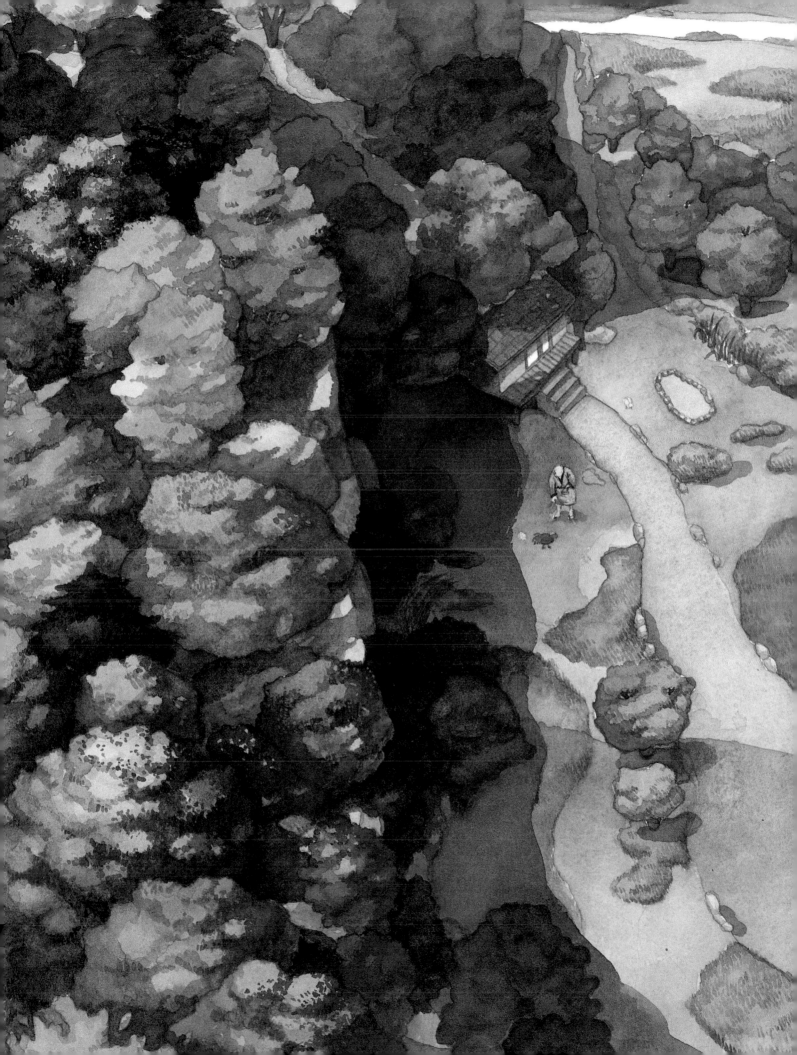

Not far from his hut a wild cherry tree grew beside a river. Its late-summer cherries were so sweet Basho could never find words to describe them.

One hot August
day, as Basho came along
the river hungry for cherries,
he saw a fox climbing down out of
the tree. Its white muzzle was stained
red from the many cherries it had eaten.
"Kitsune!" Basho yelled. "Leave those
cherries alone! Scat!"

The fox stopped and looked Basho over. "The crows told us a poet had come to live around here. You must be the one."

Basho bowed proudly.

"And you think you deserve these delicious cherries all for yourself?" the fox continued haughtily. "I'm afraid I can't agree.

"We foxes are far better poets than humans are. In fact, some of the best poems humans know were actually whispered to them as they slept, by foxes. We've given you our leftover poems—and you think they're masterpieces! I'll eat these cherries whenever I feel like it." The fox turned to go.

I had no idea foxes were such magnificent poets! Basho thought. "Wait!" he called. The fox turned around.

"I'm no ordinary poet," Basho said with quiet pride.

At that the fox sat back on its haunches and looked interested. "A *great* poet, eh? Well, there's something here after all! Very well, great poet. I will discuss this matter with you in the spring." With that the fox trotted off, its nose in the air.

All winter Basho ate his food, slept his sleep, lived his life, and wrote his poems. And from time to time, struggling to stay warm on his thin sleeping mat, he felt his mouth watering at the thought of late-summer cherries.

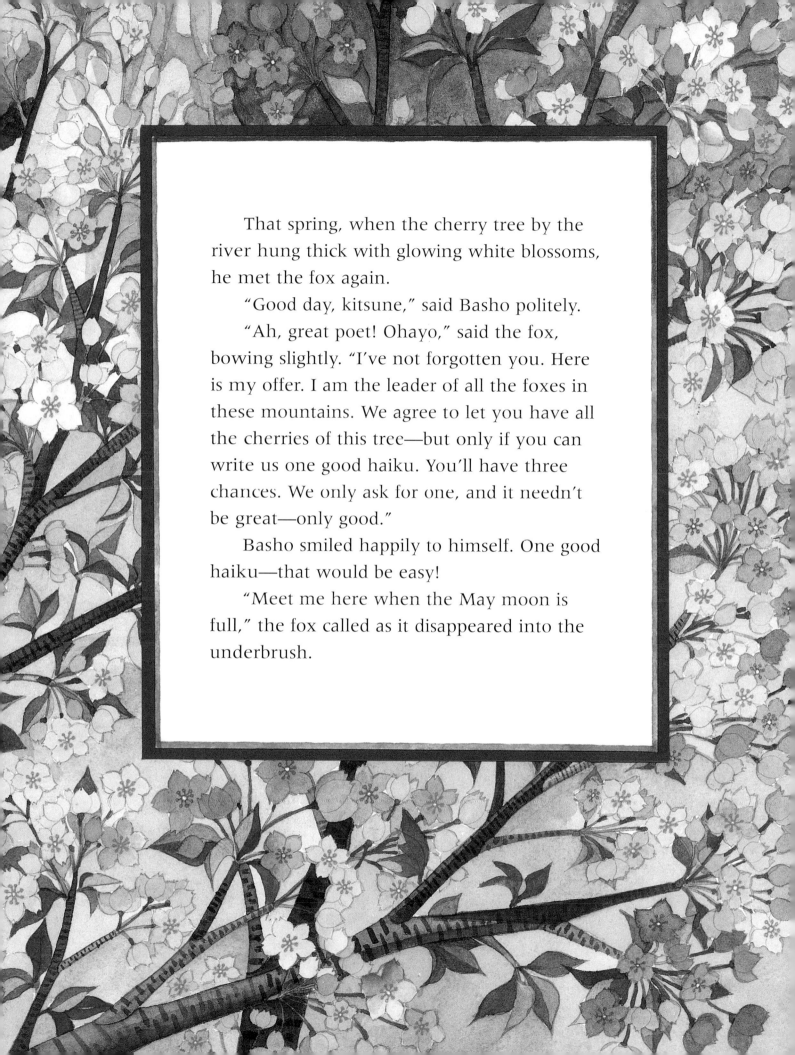

That spring, when the cherry tree by the river hung thick with glowing white blossoms, he met the fox again.

"Good day, kitsune," said Basho politely.

"Ah, great poet! Ohayo," said the fox, bowing slightly. "I've not forgotten you. Here is my offer. I am the leader of all the foxes in these mountains. We agree to let you have all the cherries of this tree—but only if you can write us one good haiku. You'll have three chances. We only ask for one, and it needn't be great—only good."

Basho smiled happily to himself. One good haiku—that would be easy!

"Meet me here when the May moon is full," the fox called as it disappeared into the underbrush.

For a month Basho worked, writing new poems,
reading old ones, searching for a haiku so beautiful

and powerful that the old fox would be amazed.

When the full moon came he went to the cherry tree.
The fox was already there, sitting silent on the grass.
Basho bowed and then recited in the moonlight:

*With the scent of plums
on the mountain road—suddenly
sunrise comes!*

For a while there was no sound except the burbling of the river over its stones. Then the fox stood up.

"My friend," it said with pity, "you have a long way to go before you can call yourself a poet! Meet me at the next full moon—if you have something better."

As the kitsune slipped away into the shadows, Basho stood there stunned. A long way to go?! *Then even my best poems aren't good enough for the foxes!* he thought. He walked home with a lump in his throat, paying no attention to the moon.

But his sadness soon gave way to determination. *I am a great poet!* he told himself.

So he worked for another month, writing and
re-writing, changing words and adding words and taking
words away, reading and listening and considering.

When the moon was full again, he went to the cherry
tree and found the fox waiting. The poet bowed, closed
his eyes, and recited his haiku:

An old pond.
A frog jumps in.
The sound of water.

But when he opened his eyes, the fox had already turned to go. "A little better," it called over its shoulder, "but our pups can do as well as that. You have one more chance."

For the next month Basho worked even harder at his haiku, letting poems flow into him and out of him, then polishing them till they seemed perfect. But when he finally looked over all the new poems he'd written —he didn't like any of them!

At last came the night of the full moon. Wondering which poem to take, Basho felt nervous and confused. As he sat over his papers he noticed the moon was already high. So he left his hut and hurried to the cherry tree without any haiku at all.

Maybe I can make up a good one before I get there, he told himself. But his mind just wouldn't work. All he could think about was the embarrassment he'd feel standing before the fox with nothing to recite.

As before, the fox was waiting, the red of its fur pale in the moonlight. "This is your last chance," it said in a bored voice.

What now? Basho asked himself wildly. He looked over at the fox and then up at the great white moon. Suddenly a haiku came into his head, as easily as flowing water. *It's not really a good one,* he thought, *but at least it's something. . . .*

Summer moon over
mountains is white as the tip
of a fox's tail.

The fox gasped, rising suddenly. "Ahhh! Sensei, forgive me! I had no idea you could write such...such a perfect haiku! These cherries are yours forever! Please—say it one more time!"

Basho felt dizzy with confusion, but he recited the poem again. The fox sat with its eyes closed, savoring the words as if they were ripe cherries. At last he opened his eyes and said, "Now I must run back to my family—just wait till they hear this one!"

"But *kitsune*—please!" Basho said. "Why do you like this one and not the other two? What's so good about this one? "What a silly question!" the fox called back as it scampered off along the river. "This one has a fox in it!"

From that day forward, Basho understood that a poem should be written for its own sake—and that the foxes of Fukagawa were not such great poets as they thought they were.

But he shared the late-summer cherries with them anyway.